KU-691-191

Which I am afraid cannot be said for
Little Miss Whoops.

She also loved to dance, but she was not elegant.

And she was not graceful!

Poor Little Miss Whoops, how she wished she could
dance in a real ballet.

Please return / re~ ~ date show~

~ar

ATT /~

MR. MEN
Ballet Show

Roger Hargreaves

Hello, my name is Walter. Can you spot me in this book?

EGMONT

It will come as no surprise if I tell you that Little Miss Somersault was good at somersaults.

But somersaults were not all that Little Miss Somersault was good at.

She was also good at ballet.

She loved to dance.

She knew all the ballet positions.

She was so elegant and graceful.

So, when Little Miss Somersault decided to stage her own ballet Little Miss Whoops was one of the first to arrrive for the auditions.

Little Miss Somersault watched her perform.

She was, of course, not very good.

Little Miss Whoops landed on her nose when she tried to pirouette.

Whoops!

Little Miss Somersault shook her head.

"I am sure that you can teach me," pleaded
Little Miss Whoops.

Little Miss Somersault could see how much Little Miss
Whoops wanted to learn and she was sure that she
could teach her to dance, so she gave her a part in
the show.

And so the week of rehearsals began.

Although things did not begin well.

Mr Wrong wore the wrong shoes.

Little Miss Naughty got up to her usual tricks.

Mr Muddle painted the stage floor rather than the stage set.

And Little Miss Bossy was such a bossy conductor that the orchestra were too scared to play.

But slowly the production came together.

Everything was going well.

Everything, except for Little Miss Whoops' dancing.

As hard as Little Miss Whoops listened to Little Miss Somersault's instructions she just could not make her feet do the right thing.

Little Miss Somersault did not know what to do.

Little Miss Whoops was to perform the finale.

A hug from Little Miss Hug made Little Miss Whoops feel a bit better.

And Little Miss Somersault just had to hope that it would be all right on the night.

The night of the big performance arrived.

Everyone came to see the show.

Little Miss Princess sat in the Royal Box.

And Little Miss Splendid had to sit in the not quite so Royal box next to it.

The curtain rose and the production began.

Everything went to plan.

And then it came to the finale.

It was Little Miss Whoops' moment.

She was very nervous.

As she stepped onto the stage, her bandage caught on a nail, which made her spin round.

And as her bandages unravelled she span faster.

And faster.

And faster!

She crossed the stage like a spinning top.

And came to a stop in the middle.

With a great roar of approval the crowd rose to its feet with a mighty cheer.

They had never witnessed such an extraordinary pirouette.

"Bravo!" cried Little Miss Somersault.

Little Miss Whoops curtsied and…

…fell flat on her face.

Whoops!